TIGER SOUP

A Richard Jackson Book

An Anansi Story from Jamaica

retold and illustrated by

FRANCES TEMPLE

Manufactured in the United States of America. Printed by Barton Press, Inc. Bound by Horowitz/Rae. Book design by Mina Greenstein. The text of this book is set in 16 point ITC Barcelona Medium. The illustrations are torn and painted paper collage. 10 9 8 7 6 5 4 3 2

Library of Congress Cataloging-in-Publication Data. Temple, Frances. Tiger soup : an Anansi story from Jamaica /retold and illustrated by Frances Temple.   p.   cm.   "A Richard Jackson book"— Half t.p. Summary: After tricking Tiger into leaving the soup he has been cooking, Anansi the spider eats the soup himself and manages to put the blame on the monkeys.
  ISBN 0-531-06859-5. ISBN 0-531-08709-3 (lib. bdg.)
  1. Anansi (Legendary character)—Legends.   (1. Folklore—Jamaica. 2. Anansi   (Legendary character))
I. Title. PZ8.1.T256Ti 1994 398.24'52544—dc20   (E) 93-48834

with help from Annette, Maureen, Denzel, Ariella, Ethan, Derek Luke, Josephine, Laura

TIGER SOUP

Daisy, Forrest, Lauren, Tyler, Katie, Walter —

Tracy, Carola

Orchard Books · New York

It's a fine day, down by the side of Blue Hole, and Tiger is cooking. Tiger has a fire, and he has a pot, and in the pot he is putting everything that can make a soup delicious.

Tiger is stirring the soup with a big spoon. From time to time he takes the spoon from the pot. He sticks out his pink tongue, shuts his eyes, and tastes the soup.

"*Mmmm,*" he says. "This soup needs— Coconut!"

Tiger scatters in coconut. He slowly takes another taste.

"*Ooo!*" he says, shaking his head. "Better, better, better! What about I put some— Fresh mango!?"

Tiger chops the mango, flings it in.

"*Ahhh, yes,*" says Tiger, sniffing the steam. "This is sweet soup now. Maybe just some little pinch of— Nutmeg?"

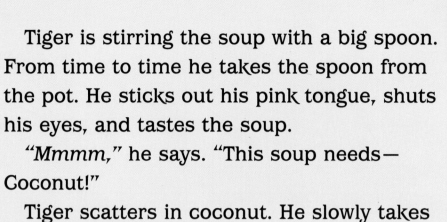

Now along comes Anansi, dancing through the forest. His nose in the air, sniffing the breeze.

"*Hmmmmm!*" says Anansi. "I smell sweet soup." And he rubs his belly. "Soup time, Anansi, m'dear. Hi-*hee!*"

Anansi swings out of the woods. Lands just beside Tiger.

"Oh! Brother Tiger! Such a happy surprise to see you here. And you so busy working, m'friend!"

"I'm just cooking, Brother Anansi. Is nothing but a little soup to satisfy the working man hunger."

"Yah!" says Anansi. "I'm not so fond of soup myself. . . . Sure is hot today, not so, Brother Tiger? Nothing in the world so nice as a swim in Blue Hole on a hot day like today."

"I'm not a swimmer, Brother Anansi, so I wouldn't know about that."

"Ah," says Anansi, shaking his head. "Such a shame to live your whole life near Blue Hole and never take a swim. . . . You want me to teach you to swim, Brother Tiger? Is always a pleasure to help a friend."

"Well, Anansi, is that I do appreciate the offer, but right now I was planning to eat some soup."

"That soup?" says Anansi. "That soup looks mighty hot and nasty, Brother Tiger. That soup will burn your tongue, m'friend."

"Let me just wait, then," says Tiger. "Soup will cool."

"You know," says Anansi, stretching his legs this way and that, "swimming in Blue Hole like magic. . . ."

"How's that, Brother Anansi?"

"Swimming does make plain ordinary soup taste like angel soup, Brother Tiger."

"The soup already delicious, Brother Anansi," says Tiger.

Tiger is thinking, How am I gonna get shed of this lazy fellow so I can eat my soup?

Right then, Anansi says, "Brother Tiger, I am bound and determined to teach you to swim today. Let's get started, so I can be on my busy way!"

"On your busy way, Brother Anansi? Agreed!" says Tiger.

Tiger and Anansi stand by the edge of Blue Hole.

They look down past their feet to the water.

"We close our eyes," says Anansi. "Then I count to three, and we both dive in."

"Right," says Tiger, and he shuts his eyes tight. "We close our eyes. You count to three. We both jump in."

"Yes," says Anansi, one eye on Tiger, one eye on the soup.

"*ONE, TWO, THREE!*" yells Anansi.
On three, he chunks a big coconut
into the water. *SPLASH!*

Tiger, his eyes tight shut, hollers,
"Here I come, Brother Anansi!"
SPLASH!!!

"Ooooo!" says Tiger, coming up all wet in Blue Hole. "This is nice. This is fine. . . . Where you, Brother Anansi? *Ooooo*, I do like this swimming!" And off he goes, splashing and singing.

Back on shore, Anansi quick
quick grabs up the spoon to slurp
down all of the soup. Then,
fast as he can drag his fat
self, he scurries off to the
woods.

Anansi is scared of Tiger now. He sidles along over branch, under leaf, thinking and thinking, till he comes to Little Monkey Town. All the little monkeys are playing outside. Shooting nutmegs, down on the ground.

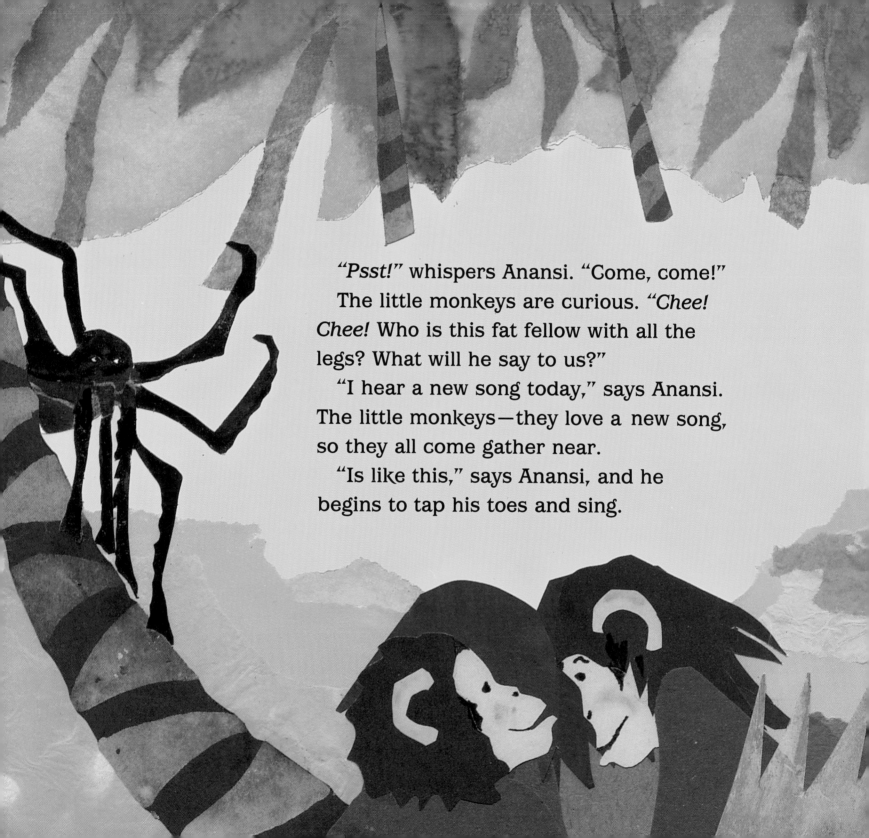

"*Psst!*" whispers Anansi. "Come, come!"
The little monkeys are curious. "*Chee!
Chee!* Who is this fat fellow with all the
legs? What will he say to us?"

"I hear a new song today," says Anansi.
The little monkeys—they love a new song,
so they all come gather near.

"Is like this," says Anansi, and he
begins to tap his toes and sing.

"Just a little while ago
We ate the Tiger soup!
Just a little while ago
We ate the Tiger soup!

"Try it, little monkeys!"
And they do.

Pretty soon all the little monkeys
are dancing and singing with
Anansi, beating sticks together,
shaking shells, making that
song a *song*.

So Anansi, leading the dance,
quick thinks up another verse:

"Yum yum yum yum yum
Taste that coco-nut!

"Yum yum yum yum yum
Taste that coco-nut!
Yes!"

Brother Anansi is so full up with soup, he
can dance no more. Not only he tire, he fit
to die laughing. Anansi falls down on his
back, all his little legs in the air, and goes
right on singing:

"Yum yum yum yum yum
Little bit o' sweet mango
Yum yum yum yum yum
Little bit o' sweet mango!"

Anansi feels a thump come up through the ground. Seems like he hears a roar in the woods.

The little monkeys—they so busy dancing they hear only the song. Anansi calls to the little monkeys, "One more time now, little monkeys! Sing it loud!"

And they do.

"JUST A LITTLE WHILE AGO
WE ATE THE TIGER SOUP! . . ."

Just then, Tiger pokes his head out from behind a bush, and Anansi's gone. All the little monkeys there, dancing and yelling their song for Tiger alone.

Tiger's ears stand up, and his fur stands up, and his teeth stand up, and *he* stands up.

Tiger roars:

"LITTLE MONKEYS! IS ME, TIGER!
JUST A LITTLE WHILE AGO, YOU ATE
THE TIGER SOUP, AND NOW,
THE TIGER GOING TO EAT—<u>YOU</u>!"

But in the time it takes Tiger to roar,
all the little monkeys swing up into the treetops,

where they been living safe, safe
ever since.